TARGET

POEMS

KATE EVANS

ALSO BY KATE EVANS

MEMOIR
Call it Wonder: An Odyssey of Love, Sex, Spirit, and Travel

NOVELS
For the May Queen
Complementary Colors

POETRY
Like All We Love

NONFICTION
Negotiating the Self: Identity, Sexuality and Emotion
in Learning to Teach

TARGET

Poems

Kate Evans

Coyote Creek Books | San José | California

ISBN: 978-1-946647-16-0

Cover art by Nancy Larrew

Printed in the United States of America

Published by Coyote Creek Books
www.coyotecreekbooks.com

For Dave

And many thanks to
Paul, Jan, Nancy, Collin,
Anne, Persis, and Shirindokht

"Above the Town" and "Living Room" previously appeared in *poemeleon*.

"Elephant" previously appeared in *Alehouse* and *Verse Daily*.

The poems in "First" (Section 1) previously appeared in *Like All We Love* by Kate Evans (Q Press).

"I Have No" previously appeared in *Zyzzyva* and *Elephant Journal*.

Eternity is not something that begins after you are dead.
It is going on all the time. We are in it now.

– *Charlotte Perkins Gilman*

Contents

6 / Nomad 2016-2017

1 / First

1992-2006

First

I have to die first, you say. When we met
we called in sick, ate in bed, let dishes and dust
collect. Blossoms confettied out-
side. We were like foals, newly testing

our skeletal limbs. *I have to die first*,
you say, the woman who stopped eating
when the dog died, as though feeling
your flesh wasn't yours, or didn't exist

anymore. So you think *I'm* the strong
one, the one who can stand being left.
me, the one who, alone in the house, dusts
the furniture, the remainders of our long

departed skin. The one who wipes the ghost
of our fingerprints from the mirror, who
washes our scent from the sheets, who
rinses the spoon that touched the moist-

ness of your tongue. When we were in bed
last night we imagined how we'd go. Our
favorite: I'm 100, you're 104.
Our hearts stop, just stop, gently, you said,

in our sleep. At exactly the same moment.
But we know there are likelier fates.
I have to die first, you say. And it's late,
it's late. We're drifting off, even as you say it.

Marriage

My father: he loves you like a daughter,
he told you at his bedside after he almost died.
Shortly thereafter your mother almost died,
too, but the body can be strong as water,

lapping, lapping, lapping the shore. Ten
years ago our families quaked with the thought
of our love. Like a vein in body or rock,
we can trace the pulse of change around a bend

in time. First: the earthquake. Then other
things that don't quite feel like change, but are.
Then one day we hear on the radio the mayor
saying we can marry at City Hall. Your mother

lay in bed that day, and my father's lungs were
counting time. *Do you take this woman, do you
take this woman.* Their bodies allowed them to
live long enough to turn the pages of our

wedding album. In a dark closet somewhere sit
our parents' wedding photos, men with brush-
cuts, women with umbrella dresses and plush
smiles. We've rushed into bedrooms and kitchens

fearing another fall. We've charged to ERs
our throats heart-filled. I brought her a glass of water
and your mother called me *baby*. Baby, daughter,
our parents wrapping us back in the womb

back to the moments they lay with their loves, newly
married, warm with sex. Can't you see her smooth
thin arm, his taut skin? They have years to move
the world, to see their daughters married, and to love.

Above the Town

Sometimes I like to pretend we're Chagall
and Bella, flying like kites above the town,
afloat in air like sea. Yes, the painting's fairly

water-like, greens, grays, blues, Bella's hair
buoyant, her arm drifting, her black gown
pulling down at the throat. And Chagall's

arm around her, his leg outspread—he's pulling
her ashore. *God, he is.* She has drowned,
you can see she's gone, her flat unblinking stare

and his eyes are ringed with gray. There,
can't you see? He jumped in when he found
her floating, her seaweed black hair, the pall

of her alabaster skin. Without him, she'd fall
to the town below. Fueled by overpowering
grief and love, he transforms water to air,

that's all he can do, I see now, just barely
hold on. Now I see a grave in the sky, down
and up reversed. One of us will die first.

Bed

Like your mother, we stay in bed all day.
You and I are mesmerized by skin, the way
our touch allows each other in. Every day

my mother kneels and cups her hands
on my father's back. She pounds
and he coughs and coughs, a resounding

bark to clear the lungs that will never clear.
His coughing is like crashing. We hear
him everywhere. But your mother is clear

as water, quiet as a crypt. Our house is quiet, too,
bed-hush, skin to skin. The light our window's
letting in is steady gray, as though there is no time. A rose

bush, jostled by a breeze, scratches the glass as if to say
it's time to rise. And it's true, these days
we must rise, must climb a ladder to change

the bulbs my father used to change, stand
high to wash the windows he can't wash. We bend
from our heights to kiss your mother, to hand

her food she will not eat, to count the breaths
of inhaled mists, without much breathing
left. Which one of us will live long enough

to see everyone fall away? A hundred
years from now, two others will lie in bed
in this house, if this house exists, or a ghost of this bed.

What My Father Gives

The doctors and nurses and respiratory therapists come in
with vitals and clipboards and white or black shoes, pushing

buttons like astronauts, speaking words I don't know. My father's
lungs are failing, they've been failing a long time, twenty-five

years of failing, and I've lived my whole life as though I'm not dying.
They've asked my mom to take his wedding band, to pull it off

his finger after forty-seven years, her own fingers white as bone,
his as red as the crushed velvet bedspread on my growing-up bed

in the room of our new house where Dad built the redwood decks
around the oaks to save them, the house where we had rules like draw

the drapes when the sun shines in the living room so the carpet
won't fade, like take off your shoes in the entry so you don't

track in dirt, and when that didn't work, walk only on the plastic
runners. Those runners had little rubber prongs that dug into the

carpet to stay put, and sometimes I'd turn them over and walk on the
prongs barefoot for a pleasing pinch of the feet. My sister and I

had our own rooms with big windows that looked out onto blue oak
and manzanita and ghost pine. One night I woke to an owl sitting

on a limb at my window. I turned on my light to see her better but
of course the window turned opaque. Raccoons and possums

fell into the pool, and Dad fished them out with the leaf skimmer,
its handle curving with dead weight. When he started coughing

I can see he was still young, not much older than I am now.
He drove my sister and me to school, one of us folded in the backseat

of the sports car that didn't really have a backseat. As he shifted gears
spots of coffee jumped from his ceramic mug, and the cold morning

air made his cough worse. Around then, the time of the blue sports car,
he started hooking up to a machine in the morning and again at night

then lying on a slant board for my mom to pound his back and chest
so he'd cough up the phlegm his lungs refused to clear by themselves.

He wears flannel shirts and Birkenstocks, has a full head of dark
hair, just a little gray, and a handlebar mustache they shaved in the

hospital so they could tape still the tubes. When they pulled the tape away,
when he unexpectedly lived, we saw they had shaved only above the lip

so his handlebars remained, unanchored. He has crystal blue eyes that turn
bloodshot when he coughs and coughs, and with my mom on a trip, I'm the one

who pounds him, and when we finish, cleans the machine. I throw out
the fluids still warm from his body, rinse the machine with dish soap. Then

I make him breakfast and he asks for more strawberries or hotter coffee
and a glass of water in a short glass. He knocks over the tall ones.

My mom has taken a group trip to the other side of the continent.
Dad insists on coming to the airport to pick her up, even though it's cold and late.

When she comes through the gate, her small folded body, her cloud-white hair,
I think she can see that nothing has changed, that my father still wheels his

oxygen, and they kiss. On the trip she met an 83-year-old woman
who still teaches second grade and who lives in a Manhattan apartment

and Mom is astonished that some people live their whole lives unlike us,
no backyards or garages or leaf-strewn decks. Ten years ago I fell in love

with a woman and it seemed an apocalypse, like an atomic blast cremated
the house, incinerated the formal dining room. I was stubborn. There was no

middle ground. My parents grasped at me like a kite string in fierce wind.
We married in February when the mayor of San Francisco decided

to break the law, and afterward my parents took us to dinner, held glasses
of wine, rubied in gold candlelight. When we thought he was going to die,

when his breath was like a crack in a sidewalk, my father told her
that she was like a daughter to him. I saw him holding onto that bed,

as fiercely as he lived. I have lived as though death belongs to him.
He has owned it for me. That is what he wants, I now see, my immortality.

Two Women on a Summer Morning

We're in bed. I can see as I look at the floor
that the carpet's hairy. Should we be doing more?

I could vacuum. You could write down the lyrics
of your ad-lib song that's making me hiccup

from laughing so hard. The cat's at the screen,
the dog's on her pillow. My ex-boyfriend is curing brain

diseases in his lab. Your ex-girlfriend's writing a sermon
or ministering to the poor. The cat's got worms, and

I keep forgetting to go to the vet. Your made-up song
is petering out. So is the feeling we belong

in this bed. The dog stands, yawns, circles,
lies back down. We touch hands, shift on our pillows

and we're starting to giggle at something
you've said in a Martian accent. Somewhere a phone rings,

a motorcycle roars by. Summer is lying
to us: Lounge around. Sleep some more. There is no dying.

2 / Smashed

2007

Target

When you said you wanted to leave me
we'd been together for millennia.
The news split me like a peach, bruised, rotten, gnawed on, thrown to
the
ditch
from a speeding car, to be eaten by ants,
run over by
a skateboard, bicycle, semi,

smashed. No, I wasn't a peach.
I had lungs that, although I lay smashed on the side of the freeway,
continued oxygen exchange of their own volition.

In out
      in out
           in out
like ocean waves
like a fetus's heart in a woman who doesn't know she's pregnant
and doesn't want to be.

Where was I?

Oh yes, devastation.

No longer am I the center
of someone's universe.
So that's what it's about. Egocentricity
disguised as love.

Let me get back to my bed.
I'm alone in it.
Not even an aubade.

Last night was drinks with a platonic friend. I drank
slowly and not overly much,
bantered like a 1940s character actress
with a tall young man who looked like a cross between
Cary Grant and Hugh Grant. At closing they turned up
the lights and he got a good look at
my age, and I at his. He could have been
my son if I'd conceived as a teenager. Yes, he could have been
my fetus once.

He had a large head the way
fetuses do. But don't get me wrong.
He was as perfectly white-man
handsome as a Hollywood movie star.
CNN anchor handsome, winning-politician handsome.

And me?

I wasn't that drunk for the first time in a long time
since you left me.
Maybe I'm getting a handle on things.
Maybe the handle is on the baggage I'm carrying. I seem to recall
an old TV commercial for luggage—an ape throwing around
a suitcase. Was it filled with rotting fruit?
The ape jumped on it
to demonstrate indestructibility.
You were the ape. You threw me,

a green suitcase with gold locks,
around your zoo cage. You and your new lover were gorillas
in the yab yum position, lovingly cuddling in a swinging tire
on a rope, feeding each other
old, bruised peaches.

Then you spotted me,
a green piece of luggage in the corner.

You'd forgotten I was there.
You were surprised at this battered object
with its gleaming locks.
Surprised and a little enraged.

How fun! A toy!

And the two of you
pounced, cameras rolling for the commercial.
God it was *funny*, two crazy cute gorillas
throwing around that suitcase.

Wait a minute.

What I really want to say is, fuck you.

I mean, I love you.

I mean, I loved you once. For a millennium. Except maybe
in our sixth year when I felt terribly trapped.
So trapped that I imagined you
dying of a horrible disease, but quickly.
Or getting killed in a car wreck,
freeing me to be the loving, grieving lesbian wife
who could go fuck men
in her grief.

But I never did!
I never arranged your death.
I never kissed another man
or woman. Of that I can be self-righteous! I mean
proud. Can't I?

I thought if I left you, you'd die.

How could you have left me
me
me?
Wonderful, beautiful, smart, loyal
me.

Love designed as egocentricity
and the other way around.

I know a woman whose husband told her by email
he wanted a divorce.
My rebound broke up with me by email.

We are so civilized, unlike apes.

My rebound ate my fruit (well, not really,
he didn't seem to like oral sex; but this is metaphor).
He was Eve, eating my fruit.
It felt so damn good.
Then he threw my pit out the window of his speeding car.
Here I am in the ditch again embroiled
in poisonous freeway exhaust, tossed away
with the discards of the world,
the used condoms and sugarfree candy wrappers stinking
of fetid chocolate,
ants and worms.

With all these freeway references
it's evident I'm, like, a Californian.
I'm the Joan Didion of the heart. She's still alive,
isn't she? Her husband died of a heart attack
in the living room as she made dinner
in the kitchen. Last she saw him alive, minutes before,
he'd been drinking scotch in his favorite chair
before the blazing fire. Their adult daughter languished
in the hospital
with a rare disease.

Had Joan heard a noise?
Had she encountered her husband dead
(or nearly so)
on the floor when she walked in with a fresh drink?

The solid fantasy of life-long marriage
liquefies just
        like
           that.

He was dead, or unrevivable, when the paramedics arrived.
She wrote a book about it. Then her daughter
died. The only parallel I can think of is biblical.
Joan Didion as Job.

Why does an atheist go biblical at times like these?

Let me try transcendentalism, to ponder infinity in leaves
of grass. Walt's been dead a long time—both
Whitman and Disney. I used to love
Tinkerbell, sitting cross-legged in my footie pajamas,
my head tight in curlers
woven into my bath-wet hair by Mom.
Tinkerbell waved her magic wand over the magic kingdom,
and all those sparkles fell onto the world.

Is that what I did with us?

Fetishize the sparkles?

I told and retold the story of how we fell in love.
You, my first woman. Unless you count the crush
I had on my gynecologist—
mutual, I believe, because she called me at home to see how
my bladder infection was doing.
What doctor does that?
I listened to her voice over and over
on my answering machine

and a shiver of something traveled from my thighs up to
my breasts, perhaps what a woman who has just conceived feels
when sperm climb up to the egg and mitosis begins.

I wouldn't know.
I've never been pregnant.

(They say women can have spontaneous miscarriages
when they think they are having a heavy period.
Perhaps a fetus disguised as a few cells
dropped out of my body a time or two.)

After you smashed me
and I finally scraped
my sorry ass off the cage floor
or side of the freeway, what have you, I had sex with a man
for the first time since I'd thought I was a lesbian.
Like teenagers, this guy and I fucked in a car,

shotgun seat, drunk, so late at night it was almost morning,
overlooking the ocean, no condom. I hadn't felt
that good since I fell in love with you
and we spent two months
in bed
(we were teachers, it was summer).

He was
sweet. He kissed me first, for a long time, and he knew
I was a lesbian.

He asked me, What do you want?

I said, You know.

Or maybe I said, Everything.

Or perhaps, Not to be smashed.
(I wasn't referring to drunkenness.
I was referring to heartbreak. I thought sex
might fix that.)

So his penis entered me
and I enveloped it. It seemed I was dreaming
because after millennia
of loving you
and resenting you
and having crushes on men
I couldn't believe it was real.

When I say he was tiny, I'm not
exaggerating. He was short and skinny,
jockey short and skinny—and for a reason.
He was a jockey.
You know I'm a big girl. Standing,
he came to my shoulder.
            All night we'd been sitting on bar stools
and then we were horizontal in the car.

As we'd flirted and flirted he
(Mr. 105-pound, five foot-two jockey with the face of Robert DeNiro)
told me he could climb anything.

So I was his
       mountain
              his ladder
                     his stairway to heaven.

Didn't Romeo climb a balcony to get to Juliet?
Tony a fire escape to Maria?

Mr. Jockey was ten years younger than me and so little
he could have been my Oedipal son. He climbed my mountain
with the ferocity
of a jockey racing to the finish line.

I take that back.

He wasn't in a hurry. He was so strong the bruises
lasted for weeks.
I've heard it said that jockeys are walking talking penises.
Or was that *dicks*?
Well, he seemed sweet.

And he knew what he was doing.

It had been forever since I'd been with a man and
for a moment I believed
they all might have this capacity.
I should have known someone who can
do it five times in a night is not
average.

He's a man who rides his motorcycle 150 miles an hour
who smokes cigarettes like lung cancer is a fantasy
who's anorexic and bulimic because that's what jockeys are.

I always thought my first anorexic would be
a woman.

I'd like to say I never had unsafe sex again
while I was resowing my wild oats. After being smashed
in the gutter and having turned my back on death's door
in the ICU for broken hearts,
I thought I wanted to live!

But maybe I wanted to die.

I was as reckless as the motorcycle-speeding
chain-smoking, vomiting jockey. That's what my beautiful doctor's eyes
intimated the other day when I mentioned my unsafe sex
and she ordered tests. I'd gone in

for a bad cold
and wasn't prepared.

My broken heart galloped like a horse around a racetrack.

This was a different doctor,
not the doctor I'd had a crush on years before,
and she looked like Sleeping Beauty
with porcelain skin and raven hair. I expected
chirping animated birds to land on her lab-coat shoulders.

Wait, I'm getting my princesses mixed up.

I wouldn't have minded kissing her like a prince,
extracting the piece of poisoned apple.
But she was *my* prince when she emailed me the next day
with a tone of electronic relief: *Good news! All negative!*

One time in life when negative is positive.

What I'd thought would be pure joy
was an outbreath of skeletal air. I bought the
biggest box of condoms Target carries.
I'd been to Target the previous week to buy a
pregnancy test because my loyal period was six days late
for the first time in millennia. I don't care how often
(or in our case seldom) two women breed, they can't procreate.
No unexpected fetuses in my old world.

The girl checker—

who could have been my daughter or granddaughter, my fetus or

grandfetus—

lifted the gargantuan condom box

from the conveyor belt with her plum fingernailed hand

and ran it across the scanner. I'd neglected to buy another item,

one to disguise the fact I was a nymphomaniac,

albeit a responsible one.

The detractor could have been, say, a package of sugarfree gum.

A poisonous can of air freshener. Maybe a flat-screen TV

that will live forever

in a landfill. But those items were, like,

a waste of living time.

This box was going to save my life.

This box that the purple-fingernailed, fairy tale goth princess

in a red Target smock dropped in an environmentally unfriendly

plastic bag. Why do I always forget to bring my canvas bag

into Target? Maybe canvas in Target seems like a drop in the bucket,

a flea on a horse or an ape, since the whole

corporate consumer capitalist culture

is poisoning everything anyway.

So there was the horse-size, ape-size box of condoms

in the bag and the goth princess told me how much I owed.

Inexpensive for a life saving device.

I put it on my credit card
since this divorce is ruining my finances.

I figured I'd put condoms in my purse
and next to my bed. After I'd picked up a guy at a bar once
(maybe this happened more than once)
and went home with him, or he with me—and we started making out I
said,

Do you have a condom?

He looked at me like I was a big-screen TV
tuned to PBS.

Why don't men carry condoms?
They used to in the 1950s, didn't they?—
always one in the wallet. And while that rubber might have been
decomposing
for years, and broken apart embarrassingly
when they tried to slip it on,
at least they made an attempt before their
virginal, sexed-up girlfriends fucked them anyway, and then the girl felt
that

zing from crotch to breasts and the fetus commenced,
instigating the shotgun wedding, the unwed mother's home,
an underground abortion

or a couple of months of jumping off a chair
or trying to throw herself down the stairs
to activate a miscarriage disguised as a heavy period.

In his bedroom, the bar guy
had no condom, apparently, so I pulled one from my purse.
He looked at me like a Baptist minister and said,

Why do you have that?

I said, Because I'm a sexually active woman.

Or maybe, Because I'm (not) an idiot.

Or perhaps, Because even though I'm drunk, I don't want
the sperm of a stranger
to kill me or start a new, unplanned life inside me.

We never used it because he was nothing like
the jockey. He couldn't get it up.
That's what I'm learning during the revivification of my wild oats:

When you meet men in bars they are often big drinkers
and they can't get it up. They try to not blow their cover
with inventive use of their tongues and fingers.
I could have stayed a lesbian for that. This guy had toys

—not the kind you buy at Target, but the kind you buy
at Good Vibrations.
These toys were stashed under his bed so it must not have been
the first time he went limp as soft, bruised fruit. He
pulled out one of the toys and got started on me. I was impressed
with his creativity. I always thought my first dildo job
would be with a woman.

(You and I weren't into creativity in the bedroom,
which was why we watched a lot of TV
and rubbed each other's feet.)

The guy's toy felt good
but he was only my third—or was it fifth? seventh?—
man in a millennium
and I didn't want a facsimile dick.

He asked for my phone number.

I gave it to him even though I didn't want to
because he was a child who lived in a dirty house
with a bunch of roommates.
He may have had posters on his bedroom walls
and a turntable on the floor.

In his car, he plugged my number into his cell
then my phone started to ring.

I picked up.

It was him.

I heard his voice in my right ear
and his voice in my left ear since he sat next to me
behind his steering wheel.
Bar man in stereo.
Just checking, he said, that you gave me the right number.

It had never crossed my mind not to. See, I'm very very new
to this dating thing. He called
and texted a few times, later.

What I'd forgotten—what I'm relearning—
is that the ones you don't want to call *do*
and the ones you do, *don't*.

Like this Cary Grant-Hugh Grant guy last night. He didn't
ask for my number when the lights went up
and we saw
each other's age.
If he'd asked for my number, he never would have called.
I doubt he needs toys in bed. Then again,
he was a drunk. A smart, handsome drunk. Maybe
a serial killer. Ted Bundy was Hollywood movie star, CNN anchor,

winning-politician handsome. Like Johnny Depp
with a strangling habit. My only habit

now—now that my married lesbian habit
has been crushed like a jockey's empty cigarette pack—
is the habit I bought for Halloween.

I'm going as a nun in a short black skirt and red lacy bra
and a crucifix the size of Jesus. Nuns are forced
to marry Him as part of their hazing. Do they

really want a wedding night with Jesus? Maybe they prefer
their own toys,
or the hand of a woman. The party is at the home
of my best friend from high school
who is now a gorgeous rich woman. She's never had a viable fetus
in her either. She lives in a gargantuan house
filled with edgy modern art and lunar furniture. In high school
we dated two guys

who were best friends, and Jewish.
We spent a lot of our shiska dating lives
chasing Hollywood movie star, CNN anchor, winning-politician-
handsome Jewish men. We were sixteen
and at a kegger party,
red plastic cups in our hands.

She said, If things don't work out
with our boyfriends we can become nuns.

You used to joke you had a nun sexual fantasy. I always joked
that one Halloween I'd dress as a nun so you could live that fantasy

but we always watched TV
gave out candy to trick-or-treaters
drank a bit too much wine
then fell chastely into bed. Marriage is for those
happily or miserably complacent.

Was I complacent?

Had I been happy
                         or miserable?

We fought so hard for Marriage Equality
(and the shadow side, Divorce Equality)
that when it arrived
(before California voters took it back)
we decided to make our iconic millennial
partnership heterosexually, iconoclastically legal.

I had a horrible cold
on our wedding day, and you had shingles, and we had nice outfits
and I wore makeup for the first time in, yes, a millennium.

Forty of our
closest co-conspirators joined us on
a perfect day
on a perfect boat
on the perfect Pacific, off the coast of a perfect town,
one I thought we'd retire to when I believed we'd grow old
and die together—
me at 100, you at 104,
when our hearts would stop at exactly the same
moment as we slept, holding each other in bed. You took

handfuls of Motrin because of the shingles, and I gulped down
cough syrup because of the cold, and our nephew (who is now
yours only) played the guitar and sang a sentimental, hip emo
song with his bangs in his eyes. My mom's Alzheimer's had not yet

progressed so much. She basically knew
what was happening. She had that halo
of white hair and the same dress she'd worn to Dad's funeral.
We'd hoped her confusion was grief.
On our wedding day, announced wife and wife,

Mom cried. Maybe she remembered in the recesses of her
diseased brain her own wedding, her tiny waist and circular
white skirt and plush red lips
and her brand new husband in his white jacket,
hair shiny as his shoes. A marriage that lasted

forty-nine years and now she sat on a boat deck
watching her daughter marry a woman who felt like another daughter.
We were the beloved women who lived a domestic life in a house
where your mother died in a hospital bed in the spot
in the living room
where we placed our couch when we moved in,
the location where we rubbed
each other's feet
in lieu of sex.

Our wedding night was sexless
what with the shingles and cough and drunkenness. I'm not like
drunk men. I perform very well when drunk. I think I scare
people with my enthusiasm. Even the jockey after the initial thrilling
first ride
became a halfhearted participant the second encounter.
I'm beginning to wonder if there's something wrong

with me.
Or is it environmental?
All these men poisoned by bad water
and medicated with Viagra
(if I'm lucky).

Are non-medically assisted erections a thing of the past?

Or is it that I was decades younger the last time I had sex with men,
all of whom were younger too and needed no erection assistance?

I know it.
It's me.
I'm poison.
I'm poisoned, like Mother Earth.

These men see me there in lacy bra and panties,
armed with a condom, and I'm
their best dream and worst nightmare.

Men like to keep dreams dreams.

Male sexual bravado is just that.
Spouted by automatons, fingers on keyboards and genitals.
Relationships are like email, impossible without technology.
When I dated men in the first round of my life
the internet didn't exist. The whole world of technology exploded
while I was rubbing my lover's feet and passing out
Halloween candy
in lieu of being a sexy nun.

The new man watches internet porn all the time, doesn't he?
While he should be doing other things
like living life
or making love to his wife.

He watches huge screen-sized plushly lipsticked lips
enveloping a natural or artificial dick. Women being gang banged,

women gang banging. Piercings. Tattoos. Women drinking cum like
thirsty drunks with flasks of vodka.
Body parts in motion
like a horse race on TV.

We've cum a long way, baby,
since buying a *Hustler* at a convenience store
along with a detracting Heath bar or pack of sugarfree gum.
All this free private porn and men don't need sex
with another person so much anymore.

Me? I want a real person.

I like sex. And connection. And intimacy.
Am I in trouble?

Whereas, as one of my men friends said,
when you're having sex with a man, after he climaxes
his next thought is
that he wishes you were a pizza.

This is the same friend—sweet, gay, rotund, hairy, in his 50s—
who said, Honey, you need to get out there and find the right guy
because you are at your peak
like a perfectly ripe peach
and in ten years you're going to look like me.

Is that really my life now that you've left me?
The law of diminishing returns?

I need more Walt Whitman. I need to loaf,
to chew a leaf of grass, to lose a few blades down my blouse
into my lacy bra.

Soon enough, we all become the soil. I will join
my father there. It's light now, my friend was saying,
and one day it will be dark. My little smashed fruit body
will decompose.

We could go Romantic here. Transcendentalist.
We could say I will enrich the soil for a new fruit tree.
Or a rose. But who knows?

I thought we'd die together, in bed, at 100 and 104.
My death fantasy. Maybe you will die fast of a horrible disease
after all. Or a car crash.
Maybe I will. Tomorrow.
Or maybe we will die
at the exact same moment:
me 100, you 104
in bed, holding other lovers,
or alone:
in beds across town or across continents.

3 / I Have No

2007

I Have No

children, I will have no children.
Sperm have swum in me but drowned, nothing
planted, nothing caught. I will never feel a knee

swipe across my body from the inside
like a credit card in a slot, like a dancer's toe
across a gleaming floor. My blood will never pulse

with another living heartbeat. I will never grow
blue crooked veins from baby weight. My legs
will always be less like my mother's, more like my father's.

Perhaps I will always be more child than adult,
always a daughter, never the monarch, never the queen
commanding my subjects, never the woman warm

in bed with the child who carries her dreams to me in
the blackest moments of night. I will never rush my child,
swollen, hive-ridden, to the emergency room. I will never

wonder where she is at 2 a.m., will never worry about her
drinking and driving, will never be told to fuck off
by the teenaged version of the baby

whose lips used to pull at my nipple, my milk
dropping low through my breast like love.

ON WHAT WAS ONCE LOVE

The environmentalist of your soul is alarmed.
You thought hate had disintegrated,

ecofriendly. Hulking polar bears, uninitiated,
can't get a foothold. A few fringe lovers

declare conspiracy. A tangle
of synthetics in the sea appropriates

the mounting waters. You create
greenhouse gasses, neglect to separate

your recyclables. You haphazardly debate
the cavities, the virtues, of belief and disbelief.

Your car gets horrible mileage. In the park you retrieve
a plastic bottle from the garbage like the homeless.

Where are the landfills? What feels more formless
than an inconvenient truth? Which is the best bitter pill

they make? Of the chemicals interred in your soil,
which will nourish, which poison? We forget what is most

biodegradable is the body, eyeballs to bones.
Embalming chemicals are meant to sustain

a façade of self. Steel coffin, we try to retain
the unsalvageable. Dropped deep in dirt, it's dark.

We pretend all will keep, even worm and hook
in that cool murky world of enough, and time.

The Yellow Wallpaper

Once there was no divorce. Mom
stood in the kitchen, frosting a cake

to the bone. Once there was no
change. We were chastened by fake

fingernails, by too-bright lipstick.
How could we know bad from good

or pick out shadows from light? Even the
curtains hung like an executioner's hood.

In theory, we swerved from all alleys
and walked quickly down halls, skimming

the walls. All the wallpaper was sallow
and soft as our skin, made for skinning.

4 / Threshold

2008-2009

The Trip of a Lifetime

-1-

My dad has become much more spiritual
since he's become a spirit. Maybe his blue eyes

and handlebar mustache signaled he always had angel
potential. He'd been gone only three months

when, as I sat at the computer, he—
I don't know how else to put this—

came over for a visit. My body filled with
a warmth
I recognized
as him.

My fingertips froze on the keyboard.

I resisted saying, "Hi Dad!" because I worried
he'd evaporate
if I spoke or moved.

A softening cupped my heart.

He spoke
without language, filling me with this message:

Everything's fine.

Fine as in whole, as in flawless.
Fine as in don't worry—as in lovely and pure.
As fine as the sand on an endless beach
that spreads toward the undying horizon.

A few days before he died,
he said if the afterworld
was real,
he'd find a way to pinch me.

This wasn't a pinch, though. Maybe spirits
don't have fingers.

I remember Dad's fingers,
thick fingertip pads that fumbled as he
turned newspaper pages.

Yet he grasped a hammer
so resolutely that he built redwood decks in record time,
laid down railroad ties and hauled thousands of
buckets of firewood.

He'd always slide
his ring back on
after his shower, before dinner.

- 2 -

A week after the funeral, Mom and I found
Dad's wedding band
in a drawer next to the bed,
gold and round as a tiny halo.
"Toss it," Mom said.
All afternoon she'd been saying
"toss this, toss that" about most of Dad's things.

The geriatrician asked my mom:
"In what way are a rose and a tulip alike?"
Mom said: "They are not alike."
He said: "How are a watch and a ruler alike?"
She said: "They both measure time."
"A bike and a train?"
"They are both machinery."
"A corkscrew and a hammer?"
"I don't know."
He asked: "What would you do if there was a fire in your house?"
She answered: "I'd close and lock the doors."

Patient described as showing a change in cognitive status. Her husband
of 48 years passed away two months ago. She worked as a school nurse for
many years but doesn't recall when she retired. Patient is a poor historian.

- 3 -

The doctor wrote: "Patient is a poor historian."

Pablo Neruda wrote: "Love is so short, forgetting is so long."

- 4 -

Hospice literature says:
"One week before death,
the average patient
still has
a 40% chance
of living."

It says:
"There is no medical definition
of terminal."

It says:
"There is no medical definition
of dying."

- 5 -

The next time Dad popped in for a visit
I was jogging through my neighborhood.

"Wow," he said without words, "Look, look,
look, look, look!" As my feet metronomed

on the pavement, the colors brightened. And I saw
through new eyes the crystalline winter day,

the razor-sharp infinite blue of sky, and the
fuchsia blossoms as unabashed as the sex of

the world. Mom gave me the same gift once:
a ViewMaster in my Christmas stocking.

I'd spent hours peering in,
atingle at the Wonders of the World in 3D—

azure seas and golden windows, lush veils and drapes
and rushing waterfalls—places my mother dreamed of.

- 6 -

Mom began to leave long before she died.

Her language left word by word
as though she were packing a suitcase.

She hadn't spoken in almost a year.

But when I showed her my engagement ring—
sapphire blue like my father's eyes—
she reached out and touched my face.

She doesn't visit.

I can still feel the release
of her last exhalation, like the lift of a plane.

She's off on the trip of a lifetime.

Elephant

To feel the smooth skin of water on your back
to wash the hill-dry dirt from your face
to dream of elephants ears spread
like the wrinkled wings of an ancient angel.
To believe in the baptism of nature
to immerse in the loss of everything—
not just your father, not just your lover
but your god. It's all
nothing in the low grass,
it's all the nothing of air.
We remember like elephants, then we are gone.
We are nothing.
We don't float away on the breath of dandelions,
we don't ascend. We land. Solid as rocks
embedded in hills, unmoving and mute.

5 / New Earth

2010-2015

The Bouquet

You know things are rough
when your therapist worries
about you. You've told her too much:

the drinking, the blasting music while
driving, the sex. You're impulsive
she says. You might, like a child

unsupervised, do something unsafe.
She's pretty, kind of a hippie,
probably a lesbian. You chafe

against her admonition. She's
like a lesbian version of your
mother. And you? Oh please,

Universe, how to know? Now
that your longtime wife dumped you
and you're dating men, how

to know? When she leans forward
her round turquoise pendant
on a leather string sways toward

you like a tiny blue earth.
Teach me what's next, you say,
now that I can take a breath

without every inch of my brain
crowded with my wife's lips kissing
her new lover. It begins to rain.

Your therapist talks. The parking lot
glistens, windshields baptized. Last night
you were happy. You drank a lot

of wine and laughed hard with a friend
about betrayal. Driving here today, you didn't
want a very loud song on the radio to end.

It's time to thank your mothers.
Each one. To gather your excesses
like an elaborate bouquet. Others

cannot tell you now. We need parents
for a short while. Time to shake
her hand. Her little world twirls.

Outside, raindrops sparkle on your sweater.
Your life is new, is yours, again. The key
slipping into the ignition never felt better.

Learning to Ski in Midlife

My first time here and everything
looks like Half Dome or Everest.
If you want to fly you need wings,

don't you? I keep thinking
about how Jung says we are
the protagonist in our own life

and an extra in a larger drama.
I'm terrified; no one cares. I'm an
exclamation point, they are a comma.

All the advice: Relax, it's like skating,
it's like steering a Ferrari. To me
it's more like avoiding breaking

something. The last thing broken in me
was my heart. And it wasn't a hairline
fracture. It was a Humpty Dumpty

divorce. But whose isn't? That man
swaying through the snow like a dance,
that woman floating down the mountain

like a kite … someone broke their hearts,
or will. Yet they don't stand still.
They explode through silky white

like robust angels claiming heaven.
When the lift swoops me up,
wings me over the white and blue,

my feet dangle into nothingness.
I pray to the mountain goddess:
Let me befriend the abyss.

I Felt a Dolphin Come to Me

"The soul should always stand ajar." – Emily Dickinson

I felt a dolphin come to me
before I saw her there.
She clicked and cawed beneath the sea
aglide with breath to spare.

She looked me sideways in the eye
her heft a soft gray stone—
she told me I can summon her
at times I feel alone.

The cobalt depths were limitless,
the wet a yielding skin.
I felt my breath reach endlessness,
my spirit spread within.

She rose through blue to blue above,
crowning sky and sea—
her perfect breath invited love
to breathe inside of me.

The Genuine Article

Walking the downtown streets of San Jose
is pentimento—the underlay of an old life
ghosting up through the new. On the day
I came to see this exhibit, first I saw my wife,

soon to be ex. We had Marriage Equality,
now we get Divorce Equality. We met
with our lawyers, and I hoped for finality
but nothing was settled. Our love was spent

like cash you give a whore or a slot machine.
We're both skinnier now, like we lifted
anchor—or is that dropped? We were queens
of the Rose Garden. We were gifted

at being an iconic couple. Sometimes I wake
to the man in my bed, touch the bristly hair
of his chest, and know that we make
our own reality. Real is hyper-real. Fair

is unfair. Change is unchanging. So I left
my ex and our attorneys to walk to the museum.
It was a crystalline day, azure sky. The shift
into spring reminded me that this was the season

she left. Last year the splendor assaulted me.
This year it sings its expectant promise, for
I am in love again, and the muse has asked me
to write a poem. Why do museums portend

church? Stained-glass colors, high ceilings, lofty rooms,
statues. Certainly God and Art have something
in common. They evoke our ecstasy, our gloom,
our confusion. They invite us to think

that mortality isn't death. In one of the paintings
a cat leans into a dog. We all wish for a peaceable
kingdom, but I think there is no place for lawyers
there. The apocalypse and the wreckage are

beautiful. San Quentin is a prison of the mind.
Dante made art of life's keen battles, and art
is now made of Dante. The inside, we find,
is the outside. When we peer in the eyehole, part

of us insists that, yes, life is a ViewMaster slide,
as hyper-real as two women divorcing, or being
a former lesbian, or—more to the point—
fifteen years of fueling a car hijacked by another

Rose Garden lesbian, or more to the point, your life
cleaved so brutally you're not sure you can live.
What you thought might have been happiness converts
to the futility of *trump loi'l*. All is deception. All can be bought,

stigmata of the heart. Still life lies. Nothing stays.
Take this spring, for instance. I step out of the
museum to a riot of birdsong, a Technicolor San Jose,
all mine. And I think about how

I woke this morning to my new lover's breath,
how sometimes I think man, man, man, man—
how pentimento is life's canvas always refreshed,
how city and art and sun promise new faith.

Valentine

I.

You make me laugh. Well, not quite make:
You spark the spirit of me, a glittering

silvery light that emerges to partake
in the creation of us. We are flowering

like the sunset colors that bloom
from our balcony. You read in the chair

near the window, the candle-lit room
fragrant from dinner. I wonder where

all this joy is leading me. My home
is expanding: It's a place, it's a feeling,

it's all the mountains we've walked up;
been ferried up; stood atop and marveled

at the blues of sky and snow; sat atop
and flowed with the force, the dazzle

of heart. And the mountains we've flown
down, scintillations of snow sparking up,

or clouds of earth expanding with the cadence
of our feet. Together we make an us

that swells like the waves. Do you see
the mermaid? She swims to you, freer

than she's ever been, and she feels your
arms are open, artfully taking her in.

II.

Breathe in the soft heat of the bed.
Your world and mine becomes
ours. We are crafted, handmade.
We've been woven amid the thrum

of a vital, kind-hearted artist,
one who tends to spirits
whole and acquiescent. My fists
unclench. I am fearless

with you. One day we sat
at the edge of the world, ocean
blooming below, holding hands,
eyes closed like a single

creature poised to take flight.
We have leapt, *haven't we?*
You and I are flush with light:
a golden flood of the body,

a communion of water and rock,
a union of fabric and thread.
The world offers us its breath.
Let's inhale. It's all inspiration.

Collision

I envision scenes before we met,
the film reel of my imagination

reversed. A flight attendant
hands you tea. At a gas station

you pump gas into a car I've
never been in. There you are,

underwater, mantas flying by.
And now you walk a faraway

path near a cliff overlooking
an infinity of sea. Now you're

in your father's shop, checking
on something too distant for

me to detect. You were an early
baby, delicate. And once you

floated in the dark, honeyed
womb, and before that the blue

unknown. Today I praise your
storied body, infused with light.

I praise the way you pour
into me, and I onto you. Life

is as minute as it is vast.
Life is as random as it is designed.

As strangers perhaps we once passed
on the street, your hand brushing mine.

Regeneration

We walk a path soft with duff, the day aglow
with light motes and insects. Redwood roots
interlace like fingers, swelling in warm growth

to shore the others up. You say this mountain
was logged, but regeneration has taken hold
a century later. It took you half a century

to find me. You were born in May, and it's
fifty-two Mays later that you stop me
in the path. You want me to see what you do:

the marvel of three baby skunks, white
and black ruffles of tail, snuffling the dirt,
blindly skittering toward us, obsidian-eyed

and clawed. You do what you do with most
animals: talk to them. You want them to know
we are happy to see them and mean them no

harm. Just months ago, I didn't know you
existed, a man who worships in the church
of the world, a man who opens my eyes to new

vision, a man who evokes the spirit in so much:
music's gold tones, the offering of my skin,
an avocado newly pulled from its limb.

You say I turn a new face to you. It's true.
With you I am an infant's first moment in air,
a dolphin emerging from the glittering

membrane of sea, a redwood seedling leaning toward light.
We are regeneration. We are walking this mountain
together, eyes open to the bright mysteries of life.

A Life of Yes

When I said yes to you I said yes
to life. Yes let's move in. Yes

take me down a snowy mountain,
yes love my body, a fountain

of joy. Yes let's odyssey.
Yes let's take the world's seas

and trees and flowers and animals
and people, people, people fully

into our hearts. Yes at the bay
I accept the blue stone. All todays

are ours. Yes: husband and wife.

All Those Visits

Most people my age want to sit by the fire,
dog at their feet. I used to think

that's what I wanted, too.

All those domestic, sexless years

all those animals
so many pets we mourned,

their ashes on the mantel.

Then my ex-wife's mother
her aunt
her other aunt
my cousin
my father.

All those visits
with flowers
        to their
        graves.

All those
    deliberations
        about loss.

Why we wanted
to hang out with death
I will never really
understand.

Did it somehow make us feel more alive?

Hands Off the Wheel

My husband sits on our couch
reading my poem.
He has loved other women but
he doesn't make art about it
and shove it in my face.

"We all have a past," he said
when a friend
called him brave.

There were things I thought I couldn't write
before. I disguised myself in fiction
to not upset
my wife.

We monitored
each other's thoughts, each other's dreams
as though we could split our minds at the seams
and spill the glistening viscera.

It's a habit I'm seeking
to unlearn.

Sometimes I think I want
my husband to excavate his brain,
drain his every desire onto the folds
of my body and covet only

me
me
me.

>"Love disguised as egocentricity.
>And the other way around."

I've been down this road before
and let me tell you,

there are potholes, speedbumps, construction crews,
cattle guards, wandering goats, stalled semis
a murderous hitchhiker or two

not to mention checkpoints guarded by soldiers
who don't speak your language.

Better keep your lights on, head up,
shoulders tense, anus tight,
hands on the wheel at 3:00 and 9:00.
Better stock up on No Doz, maybe a bump of cocaine,
a bottle of Oxy.

The
only
guarantee.

Wife, it whispers, warningly.

And there he sits, reading my poem,
my husband,
couched in his unknowable knowable
self, viscera appropriately encased
in that body I love to love.

    Everything
says the road sign
    is exactly as it needs to be.

Wife!

Oh how I suffer, buffeted, nearly sucked up
into the tornado's eye.
Declining to agonize over roadkill
declining to pop a pill
declining the machine gun burden,

I roll down the window
take my hands off the wheel.

My hair blows gold into my
damp, open eyes. And I know

      if I could wave a wand

I would create
this
very
life.

One of the Most Romantic Things My Husband Almost Said to Me

"Look," I say.
"Someone wrote a review of my book,

said she loved it.

Said, *I found her on the internet.
She's changed my life.*"

"That makes two of us,"
he said,

"I also found you
on the internet."

New Earth

Sometimes when I touch you
in our morning bed

I marvel that
You are poised
    at my openness
    looming over me   like a cat

on a windowsill
    in the moment
      of paw
        lifted
          to circumnavigate
      a flowerpot
     but not yet setting
   an absolute course.

Once Earth lost everything
but algae trapped
in dark ice

then heat broke the frost
    broke the unbreakable
      bore seas and lakes

           melted the unmeltable
       created new earth.

Sometimes cold pulls us so deep
we can't breathe. We think time
          has stopped.

Take heartbreak.
It seems ice will forever float
in our blood
that the Ice Age
of pain
is unthawable.

We spin
     like stripped tires
        in snow.
We believe
     the book's page
        cannot turn.

The cat gauges the perfect step. I sway
     my hips to you
     and we create
     new earth.

6 / Nomad

2016-2017

Nomadic Life

The promise of the novel thing
glitters like
    the world's bling.

Back to School Prayer

Lord, provide me with pithy speech,
> no gape in my blazer or unintentional
>> exposure. Make me as a cake on a sombrero

or a mask on an oyster: surplus,
> quirky, quickly inspired. Provide me
>> freedom from unease; allow pouts

to stay hinged on selfish mouths, unconsidered.
> I pray for the illumination of the overhead bulb,
>> the sturdiness of a well-built porch, the clarity

of the mapless tinker, the allure of the steamy
> meal. Ferry me into endless waves with a lust
>> for new waters and a thirst for horizon.

Home for Now

The little disappointments. I'm on the edge
of noticing your whole life. He had a sweet

demeanor but swore the Chinese couldn't
think critically or creatively. I don't speak

the language. I especially love the children
here. Two more classes tomorrow, papaya

and *jiaozi*. It's been quite humid. "Usefulness
comes from the void." We actually have a lotus

pond out the window. In the winter it's strewn
with sticks. Tiny grebes, splashes of deep green,

so much to receive. It feels like Friday. Could be
the last bastion of claustrophobia. When the

paparazzi descend, we get on the internet.
I lost the thread of the conversation. They are

too big for her to kill. Who stays off the internet
for a day? Expansion is coming. It's getting

darker earlier. I can't reveal this. It's not good
enough. I've wasted a lot of time drunk or hung-

over. Maybe I was just living. The thick air makes
my skin thin. They scrunch in fetal position as they

ride their motorbikes. It's a more laid-back style.
Carpe diem. Why do we stay alive? It was dark

when the kittens were born. One was dead.
My mother had gotten me out of bed to see.

I am doing exactly what I'm here to do. A ghost
doing the dishes. Her bun was blond but the hair

in front was white. In middle school, I didn't
understand. Our parents are dead or dying. I'm

going to worry about that? Ha! Good morning.
She's not happy. So many of us have thoughts

about shit that's not really our business. Am I
a "new experiences" whore? What's the main

risk? Trying to scare away the rats, those little
fuckers. It's filled with light. Can I see it as

excitement rather than anxiety? "Moonlight
is twice as white as frost." We stopped at

a few places for errands. It felt like I was swimming
in the humid mist. Is paranoid the right word?

Digging my hands into the clay of the moment.
During sex. While driving. While having a conversation.

Before Teaching

The washing machine swirls
our disembodied clothes and
soon I will will myself off this
warm couch and walk into a
room of fresh lives, all that
gleaming black hair, all those

                    sweet

seconds that bloom and droop like
flowers. That is how a lily is the same
as a person. Out the window someone
sweeps leaves. The lotus pond
gleams. We are making plans
for the new year

as though the calendar is a place
as though we don't inhabit a museum
as though we are making a movie.

Maybe we are.

THAT'S RIGHT

I am
so mad
wanting something
you can't
give me

Aha
I remember
I can
give it
to myself

Somewhere in Viet Nam

You sink down into the
hotel bed. I caress your back
until your sweltering skin
drifts to uneasy sleep. I'm restless

and thirsty. In the dark hot wet
night, tuk tuks

ma'am ma'am!

people peopling
the dissolving sidewalks
crouched on miniscule plastic stools
white streaks of cigarette smoke
chatter of words making me
stranger,
stares, stares

                             sharp scents swimming
in the viscous air, disorienting sparks of light
fish eyeing me from their deep-fried heads
piles of food
I can only guess at. Are you
lost in a dream in our faceless hotel

in this nameless town's
maze of streets?

I hope I can find my way back.
It seems I could
lose myself in another life
my hair stuck to my steamy neck.

As I cross another street
threading between motorbikes
an ancient miniscule woman
pulls at my elbow

leads me to a stand
lit up with washed-out color photos
like a ramshackle carnival

    passion fruit
    mango
    papaya
    unknowns

Somehow, she has access
to my brain.

I signal *okay* to the fruit, the blender
and wonder if she thinks
I'm an outsized baby:

pale skin, plump face, no language.
I squat on a kindergarten-sized chair
mosquitoes swarming my ankles.

I can't wait for that cold slide
down my throat,
walking back to you the way I came, I hope.
Feels like
       I could accidentally walk
       into another dimension.

You are a GPS and don't understand
my propensity for getting lost. But you
never insist I not wander.

She, the mind-reader with a
folded-in face
and gleaming eyes,
hands me the drink
takes what amounts to pennies. I want to pay her more

but she waves me away, turns to the next customer,
sends me off to slake my thirst

in the dark
sends me off
back to you
to our temporary bed
to our roving life.

Peace

Our bikes bump down the dirt road,
       handle-hot hands, sweat gripping
              my neck like a gecko on a wall. People run

scythes through the fields, recline
       on tile patios of brick houses,
              nap in hammocks, play cards

on low tables, cigarettes and beer.
       Kids romp in the dirt, women on cell phones
              drape laundry over bushes. As we near

a hair salon plastered with discolored
       glamour shots, a guy in a hairdresser's smock
              black pompadour bleached on top

(his hair like an elaborate cupcake)
       flamboyantly waves. We stop
              for water, watch a family beneath

a dragon fruit tree, the father on a ladder,
       crimson harvest. The grandmother
              cradles a fruit in furrowed hands

leans over the fence and offers it to me.

I thank her, touch her hand—me,

who as a child watched war on TV.

You Fall a Little Bit in Love

They're probably French,
dreadlocks, scuffed backpacks

downy shoulders, effortless faces
him on his phone looking at a map

her with earbuds, her head
        on his shoulder.

They have no idea
        how young
                they are.

World and Time

sapphire water, feet on sand
pen on paper

the marriage of skin and air

more than forty years ago
when I was a girl

on another beach
on the other side of the world

I wrote then, too, and felt
fingers of sun in my hair

the pen, suspended and electric
being the me
of me

HOUSESITTERS

When we first enter someone else's
life, I wonder how crazy we are.

Why aren't we planted in our own home
somewhere? I mean, we love to watch baseball

on TV. We enjoy a good beer. We like flowers
on the table and something in the oven

scenting the air. And oh, the dogs and cats
that live there. My last dog died eight years

ago. Maybe there's a fish to feed and berries
to be plucked in the back yard, potatoes to pull

like gems from the soil. We clip the dog to his
lead, walk the calm neighborhood, maybe pet

a horse or wave a hand at a neighbor. Afternoons
we watch the birds in the feeder. At night

we play cards pulled from the stack of everything
we own that's stored in our car. We step into

others' lives like a stream, pick through the stuff
in their drawers, try to hang a couple of shirts

in their crowded closets. I soak in the tub
before we climb into their bed, placing our heads

on their pillows. The dog snores.
Maybe I'll dream of another life

one of the many I could have lived.
Days, weeks, months later when they return

I'm a little startled
          that we must leave.

This isn't my life?

Oh, but it is.

And each time we get in the car
I watch them recede
in the rearview mirror

and something fills my blood
crawls into
my bones.

Something that feels
          like freedom.

p. 97: "Usefulness comes from the void." — Lao Tzu

p. 99: "Moonlight is twice as white as frost." — Wang Shizhen

Kate Evans is the author of *Call It Wonder: An Odyssey of Love, Sex, Spirit, and Travel*, awarded Best Memoir at the Bi Book Awards, where she was also named Writer of the Year. Her other books include two novels, a collection of poems, and a nonfiction book about teaching. Her essays, stories, and poems have appeared in more than fifty publications. She holds a PhD in Education and an MFA in Creative Writing. A former writing and literature teacher at U.C. Santa Cruz, San Jose State University and SCIC/Guangxi University in China, she now serves as a writing coach and book editor. Half the year she lives in Mexico, and half the year she travels. She blogs at *Living the Journey*. Visit her website at kateevanswriter.com.

www.ingramcontent.com/pod-product-compliance
Lightning Source LLC
Chambersburg PA
CBHW030546130626
46552CB00006B/2444